Letterland

ABc Stories

Written by Lisa Holt

Illustrator Nigel Chilvers

Based on characters originated by Lyn Wendon

About Letterland

Letterland is an imaginary place where letters come to life! The friendly Letterland characters help children to easily understand the sound and shape of letters – one of the key skills needed when learning to read and write.

Simple stories about the Letterland characters explain letter sounds and shapes, so that confusion over similar looking letters is avoided and children are motivated to listen, think and learn.

One of Letterland's keys to success is its 'sound trick'. By just starting to pronounce a character's name, such as 'a...' (Annie Apple), 'b...' (Bouncy Ben), 'c...' (Clever Cat), a child automatically says the correct letter sound. It's that simple! The combination of memorable characters and proven educational principles makes Letterland the ideal way to introduce your child to the alphabet.

For more information, including a pronunciation guide for all the letter sounds, see:

www.letterland.com

About this book

Read the part that suits your reading ability - take turns!

There are three stories in this book. Each story begins with an introduction to the character, it's shape and sound. You will then go on an imaginative adventure with the character.

Taking turns

Fluent reader 🔊

Story or rhyme featuring lots of alliterative words. Also available to download and listen to.

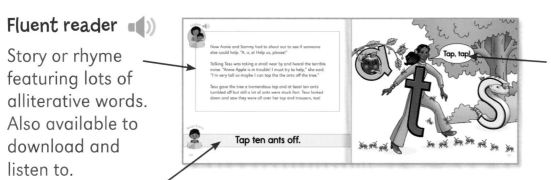

Beginner reader

These words can be read by just sounding and blending the letters into words.

t a p → tap

Early reader Sentences made up of words using the 26 letters of the alphabet in their most phonically regular form. Also included are a few carefully chosen high-frequency 'tricky' words such as 'are' and 'the' with irregular sounds. Irregular parts are in **blue**.

Note: All text is printed on a shaded background, to help those with visual difficulties.

If you would like to listen along to this book you can either scan the QR codes (pages 4, 22, 40) with a smart phone or tablet, or you can download the audio tracks from:

www.letterland.com/Alphabet-Storybooks

Scan to listen along!

With a smart phone or tablet you can download a free QR Reader from your app store. Simply scan this code, then press 'play' to listen to the story. (Fluent reader part only. 3G or WiFi connection required.)

For full details see: www.letterland.com/Alphabet-Storybooks

Published by Letterland International Ltd, Leatherhead, Surrey, KT22 9AD, UK.
© Letterland International 2013
10 9 8 7 6 5 4 3 2 1
ISBN: 978-1-86209-932-6   Product Code: TE51
LETTERLAND® is a registered trademark of Lyn Wendon.
Printed in Slovakia

Author: Lisa Holt
Illustrator: Nigel Chilvers
Editor & Originator of Letterland: Lyn Wendon
Parent/child icon © iStockphoto.com/viviyan

Annie Apple
and the ants

By Lisa Holt

Taking turns

Let's meet Annie Apple!

Listen

In an apple orchard in Letterland there is a little talking apple called **Annie Apple**.

She is a very happy little apple who is often very active appearing in lots of words. Can you hear her saying '**a**' in words like '**a**pple', '**a**nt' and '**a**rrow'?

She loves to swing in the trees like an acrobat and chat to her animal friends. Can you spot any of her friends in the picture?

One day, Annie Apple was sitting happily in her apple tree when all of a sudden she felt something moving on her back!
"A, a!" she cried. "What's that tickling me on my back?"

A little ant had landed on her head and more ants were climbing up her apple tree. She was amazed to see how many there were.

As they crawled all over her it tickled so much that she thought she may have an accident and fall out of her tree!

your turn

An ant on her back.

"Go away, ants!" she cried, but more and more arrived. Annie anxiously called out to see if anybody nearby could help her. "A, a! Help me, please!"

Soon, Sammy Snake came slithering along. "I'll save you!" said Sammy.

Sammy tried to get the ants off but the ants were all sticky and covered in sap from the tree. "It's such sticky sap!" said Sammy, sadly. "Now I've got ants stuck to my back, too!"

your turn

Lots of ants stuck on.

sap

Now Annie and Sammy had to shout out to see if someone else could help. "A, a, a! Help us, please!"

Talking Tess was taking a stroll near by and heard the terrible noise. "Annie Apple is in trouble! I must try to help," she said. "I'm very tall so maybe I can tap the ants off the tree."

Tess gave the tree a tremendous tap and at least ten ants tumbled off but still a lot of ants were stuck fast. Tess looked down and saw they were all over her top and trousers, too!

your turn

Tap ten ants off.

Now Annie Apple, Sammy Snake and Talking Tess had to shout out to see if anybody else could help. "A, a, a! Help us, please!"

Peter Puppy was playing in the paddling pool and heard the noise. He raced over. "Perhaps I can pat them off?" he panted.

He patted at the ants, but soon he had ants all over his paws. "It's pointless!" he puffed.

He cannot pat the ants off.

Then Sammy had a super idea. "It's so sunny today. Let's take a trip away from the apple orchard and go and sit on the sand by the sea where there are no ants."

"That is a good plan," said Annie. "I like adventures."

"Perfect," said Peter Puppy, as he prepared a picnic of tapas.

 A plan! Let's pack a picnic.

"Tremendous," said Tess. "I'll get us some tickets for the train."

Sammy Snake slithered off to search for sun hats and sunscreen for everyone.

They all travelled on the train together and Annie Apple quickly fell fast asleep!

When they arrived at the beach, Talking Tess gave her a little tickle to wake her up.

your turn

Sam got sun hats. Tess got tickets.

They quickly put on the sunscreen and their hats and dashed down to the water. After a lovely long afternoon playing in the sand and the sea, it was time to relax and just enjoy the sunshine.

So they did. They relaxed

and just . . .

Scan to listen along!

With a smart phone or tablet you can download a free QR Reader from your app store. Simply scan this code, then press 'play' to listen to the story. (Fluent reader part only. 3G or WiFi connection required.)

For full details see: www.letterland.com/Alphabet-Storybooks

Bouncy Ben

and his bike

By Lisa Holt

Taking turns

It was Bouncy Ben's birthday and he was very excited. "Birthdays are brilliant!" he said, as he bounced along.

His brothers had baked a big batch of banana buns and were busily setting up a birthday picnic in the park. They put up lots of bunting and brought bags full of blueberries and blackberries.

There were baskets full of brown bread baps bursting with Ben's favourite fillings and bottles of blackcurrant juice, too.

your turn

Bags full of baps and buns.

bag

bun

The brothers had also brought Ben's birthday presents to the park. They put a blindfold on Ben so it would be a wonderful birthday surprise. "I can't believe it!" said Ben. "It's brilliant!"

Ben had been given lots of presents. He got a new bag, a bright blue ball, and a book about boats. But best of all there was a big present wrapped in brown paper with a big, blue bow. Ben was bursting with excitement.

"Happy Birthday!" the brothers shouted.

Your turn

The best is a big present.

He quickly took off the big blue bow and beneath it was a brilliant new bike. But is was not an ordinary bike, this was a balance bike!

A balance bike is a very special kind of bike that doesn't have any pedals so you have to be very good at balancing.

Ben loves to balance. He can even balance balls on top of his head. But will he be able to balance on a bike?

your turn

Can Ben do it?

He got on the bike, but it was a bit tricky at first.
"Oh, bother. I'm so bad at this!" he said.
"You'll get better," his brothers replied, "just be brave."

He tried to balance but his legs kept bending the
wrong way and he bumped and bruised himself.
Poor Bouncy Ben.

He was about to give up, but his brothers told him
to get back on and try once more.

Ben bumps his leg.

This time Ben started to go down a big hill. "Come back!" they bellowed. Ben got faster and faster but...

... this time he was balancing!

"Beep beep!" he shouted, as he zoomed past Harry Hat Man and Lucy Lamp Light. Bouncy Ben beamed as he even buzzed by the bugs in the sky!

your turn

Ben can do it!

bug

"I'm balancing! It's brilliant!" said Ben.

His big brothers were on their bikes behind and they were begging him to slow down.

What Ben hadn't realised is that there were no brakes on his balance bike and now he was heading back around the bend towards his birthday picnic.

your turn

Ben cannot stop.

picnic

Buns went everywhere but...
... it was a beautifully soft and tasty landing.

"Brilliant!" said Ben, as he landed

with a big . . .

Your turn

Scan to listen along!

With a smart phone or tablet you can download a free QR Reader from your app store. Simply scan this code, then press 'play' to listen to the story. (Fluent reader part only. 3G or WiFi connection required.)

For full details see: www.letterland.com/Alphabet-Storybooks

Clever Cat

and the cake

By Lisa Holt

Taking turns

Let's meet Clever Cat!

Listen

Let's say 'Hello' to the Letterland cat. She lives in a little cottage near the Letterland castle and she's called **Clever Cat**. Why? Because she can do so many clever things. She can even count! Can you count, too?

There's another thing you should know about Clever Cat. She doesn't 'miaow'. That's because she is a Letterland cat. She makes a little '**c**' sound instead. You can hear it at the start of words like '**c**at', '**c**ar' and '**c**ake'.

Today Clever Cat has decided to bake.
She is going to create a carrot cake.

She's counts out the carrots, 1 to 4.
Flour, eggs, milk, raisins and more.

Do you think she will be a clever cook?
Let's turn the page and take a look.

Your turn

Eggs and milk and carrots.

cost

She grates the carrots into a cup,
cracks in the eggs and stirs it up.

Then there's a sudden bang at the door.
She almost drops her cup on the floor.

Annie Apple wants to ask advice,
on how to read and add up a price.

The cup of carrots tips up.

Clever Cat can make counting fun,
and shows Annie Apple how it's done.

Annie says 'thanks' and gets on her way.
Clever Cat is glad to have helped her today.

She creams the sugar with the butter.
Then cleans her paws and clears the clutter.

your turn

She can add up. It is fun.

48

Tap tap! Another knock at the door.
She puts down her cloth and stops once more.

It's Noisy Nick with some nuts in a jar.
"Look," he says, "how many there are!"

She counts them with him in a line.
Can you count, too? (There are just nine).

Next, the cat helps Nick.

51

Clever Cat chatted and lost track of time.
She didn't hear her cooker clock chime.

She had been on the phone way too long.
The cake had burnt. It had gone all wrong.

"I'm cross!" she stamped. She was really mad.
The cake was crispy and crusty and bad.

Your turn

The cat is cross. It is bad.

stamp

But you don't get a name like Clever Cat
if you cry and give up just like that.

She cut off the crust - added candy and cream.
It became the best cake you've ever seen!

If you ever get stuck, come up with a plan.
Be clever too,

we know you . . .

your turn

My Alphabet Storybooks

A 26 Alphabet Storybook pack is available from all good bookstores. For more information, including free audio downloads of all the stories, see:

www.letterland.com/Alphabet-Storybooks

Imaginative story for adult

Decodable words for child

Decodable sentence for child

Includes FREE audio

Letterland · Take turns story
Impy Ink is at the sink
Read together, read alone, read aloud!

Letterland · Take turns story
Jumping Jim is just jumping
Read together, read alone, read aloud!

Letterland · Take turns story
Kicking King and his socks
Read together, read alone, read aloud!

Letterland · Take turns story
Lucy Lamp Light likes to listen
Read together, read alone, read aloud!

Letterland · Take turns story
Munching Mike and the moon
Read together, read alone, read aloud!

Letterland · Take turns story
Noisy Nick in the night
Read together, read alone, read aloud!

Letterland · Take turns story
Oscar Orange at the docks
Read together, read alone, read aloud!

Letterland · Take turns story
Peter Puppy at the play park
Read together, read alone, read aloud!

Letterland · Take turns story
Quarrelsome Queen and her quiz
Read together, read alone, read aloud!

Letterland · Take turns story
Red Robot and the recycling
Read together, read alone, read aloud!

Letterland · Take turns story
Sammy Snake isn't satisfied
Read together, read alone, read aloud!

Letterland · Take turns story
Talking Tess and her tent
Read together, read alone, read aloud!

Letterland · Take turns story
Uppy Umbrella is so upset
Read together, read alone, read aloud!

Letterland · Take turns story
Vicky Violet and the vet
Read together, read alone, read aloud!

Letterland · Take turns story
Walter Walrus and the weather
Read together, read alone, read aloud!

Letterland · Take turns story
Fix-it Max can't fix that!
Read together, read alone, read aloud!

Letterland · Take turns story
Yellow Yo-yo Man and his yogurt
Read together, read alone, read aloud!

Letterland · Take turns story
Zig Zag Zebra and the buzz
Read together, read alone, read aloud!

Pack ISBN:
978-1-86209-861-9

See our full range at **www.letterland.com**

Goodbye from the Letterlanders!

 Annie Apple

 Bouncy Ben

 Clever Cat

 Dippy Duck

 Eddy Elephant

 Firefighter Fred

 Golden Girl

 Harry Hat Man

 Impy Ink

 Jumping Jim

 Kicking King

 Lucy Lamp Light

 Munching Mike

 Noisy Nick

 Oscar Orange

 Peter Puppy

 Quarrelsome Queen

 Red Robot

 Sammy Snake

 Talking Tess

 Uppy Umbrella

 Vicky Violet

 Walter Walrus

 Fix-it Max

 Yellow Yo-yo Man

 Zig Zag Zebra